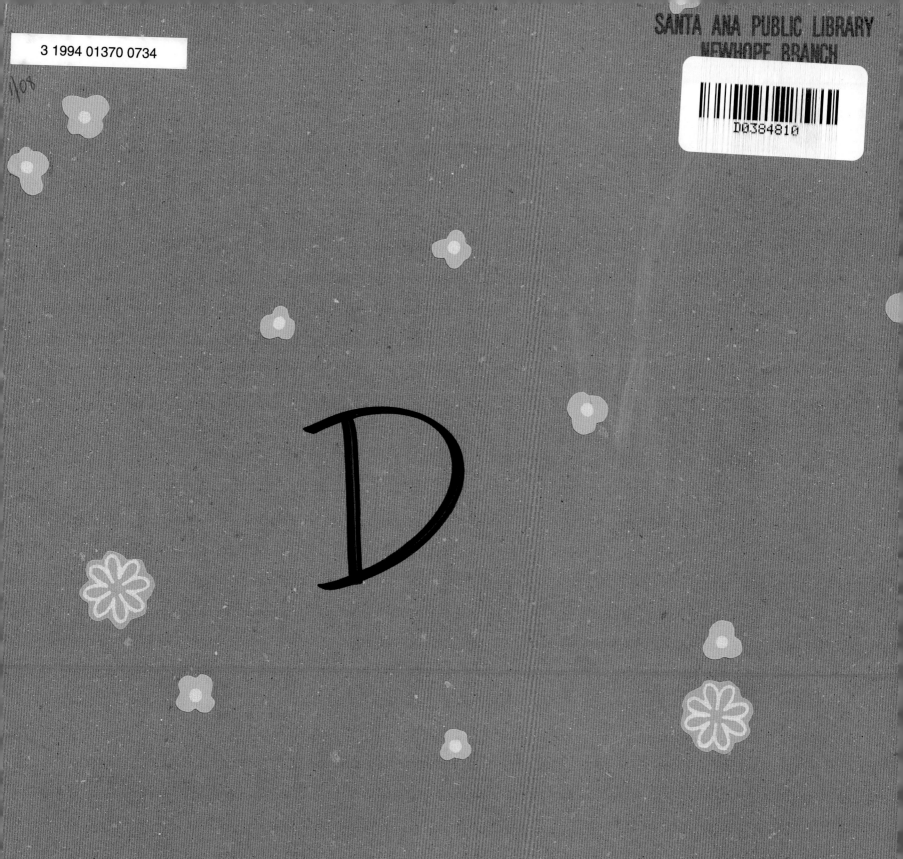

For Meg & Lucy,
Eunice's four-legged friends!

MARGARET K. McELDERRY BOOKS

An imprint of Simon & Schuster Children's Publishing Division

1230 Avenue of the Americas, New York, New York 10020

Copyright © 2007 by Caroline Jayne Church

First published in Great Britain in 2007 by Simon & Schuster UK Ltd.

First U.S. edition, 2007

The text for this book is set in Hank.

The illustrations for this book are rendered in collage and acrylic.

Manufactured in China

2 4 6 8 10 9 7 5 3 1

Library of Congress Cataloging-in-Publication Data

Church, Caroline Jayne.

Digby takes charge / written and illustrated by Caroline Jayne Church.—1st ed.

p. cm.

Summary: Digby is a very good sheepdog, but when faced with six unruly sheep who ignore him
even when he goes to extremes to make them obey, the farm's cows and pigs give him some sage advice.

ISBN-13: 978-1-4169-3441-7 (hardcover) ISBN-10: 1-4169-3441-3 (hardcover)

[1. Sheep dogs—Fiction. 2. Dogs—Fiction. 3. Domestic animals—Fiction.

4. Self-confidence—Fiction. 5. Humorous stories.] I. Title.

PZ7.C465Dig 2007 [E]—dc22 2006023973

Digby Takes Charge

Written and illustrated by
Caroline Jayne Church

MARGARET K. McELDERRY BOOKS • New York London Toronto Sydney

On the farm lived two cows, four pigs,
six silly sheep, and a grumpy farmer.

There was also a new sheepdog, named Digby.

Digby had been brought to the farm because he
was so very good at herding sheep.

"Okay, Digby," said the farmer.
"Let's see just how good you really are.
I want all those sheep
in the pen, now!"

Easy-peasy! thought Digby.
Only six sheep!

So he set to work.

But these sheep had different ideas.

They didn't like being told where to go or what to do.

This made Digby angry. He made a ferocious face
and growled at them.

But the sheep shrugged and wandered off
to eat some tasty grass.

Digby was furious and confused.

How could he possibly be a great sheepdog
if the sheep completely ignored him?

So he came up with a plan. . . .

"Into the pen, NOW!" he yelled over the noise of the engine.

But the sheep just smiled.

Digby had another idea.
"Into the pen, NOW!" he shouted
over the roar of the tank.

But the sheep weren't scared.

So he took to the skies in a huge helicopter.

"Into the pen, NOW!"
Digby cried at the top of his voice.

But the sheep simply looked up
and laughed.

Digby felt exhausted. He didn't know what to do next.
How can I be a great sheepdog if I can't even
round up six silly sheep?

He hung his head in misery.

The two cows and four pigs saw how unhappy he was.
"Come on, Digby!" they said encouragingly.
"We have lived on this farm for a long time,"
they told him. "And we've learned there is a way
to get what we want!"

They gathered round Digby and whispered their secret.

"Why, thank you!" said Digby. "Now I think I understand."

He took a deep breath and wandered over
to the sheep.
"Would you go into your pen now . . . please?"

One by one, the sheep went quietly into the pen.
And Digby never had any trouble with the
sheep again.

But the ducks were another matter. . . .

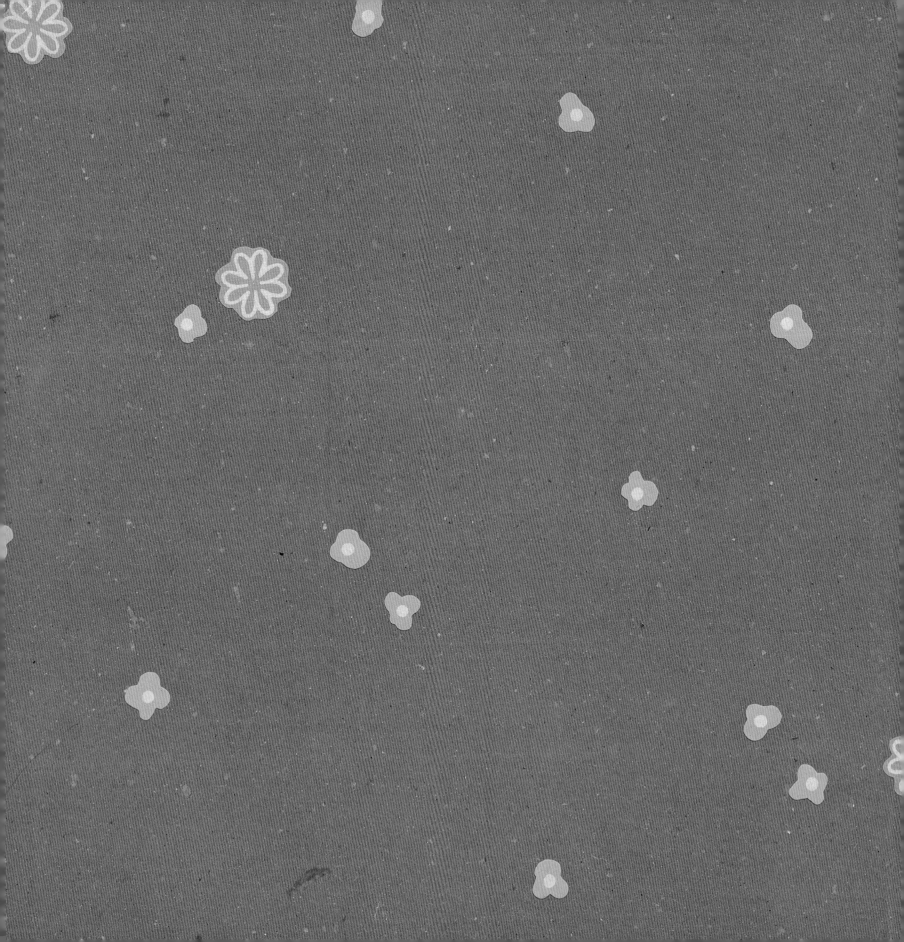